Indepe   les

Willem Samuels is the pen name of John H. McGlynn. He is a long-term resident of Indonesia, having lived in Jakarta almost continuously since 1976. He has translated several dozen books, subtitled scores of Indonesian feature films and produced more than thirty documentary films on Indonesian writers. Through the Lontar Foundation, which he co-founded with four Indonesian authors in 1987, he has brought into print more than one hundred books on Indonesian literature and culture.

Independence Day
& Other Stories
Pramoedya Ananta Toer

Translated from the Indonesian by Willem Samuels

Independence Day & Other Stories
by Pramoedya Ananta Toer

This edition has been published in 2019
in the United Kingdom by Paper + Ink.
www.paperand.ink
Twitter: @paper_andink
Instagram: paper_and.ink

The stories featured in this volume, "Independence Day" ("*Yang Hitam*"),
"Inem" and "Circumcision" ("*Sunat*") were written by the author in 1950
and first published in the collection *Cerita Dari Blora* (*Tales from Blora*,
Jakarta: Balai Pustaka, 1952). The translations that appear herein were
first published in the collection *All That Is Gone* (New York: Hyperion
Books, 2004). Minor changes to the text have been made.

The publication of this volume has been made possible with the
support of the Ministry of Education and Culture, Republic of
Indonesia, and the Indonesia National Book Committee.

Ministry of Education and Culture,
Republic of Indonesia

1 2 3 4 5 6 7 8 9 10

ISBN 9781911475415

Cover design & illustration by James Nunn: jamesnunn.co.uk | @jamesnunnar
Printed and bound in Poland by Opolgraf: www.opolgraf.com

CONTENTS

INTRODUCTION

Pramoedya Ananta Toer was born in 1925 in Blora, East Java, in what was then the Dutch East Indies. His parents were educators and fervent nationalists. In addition to raising their own nine children, they cared for up to a dozen others. Then there were the servants required to manage such a large extended family, along with assorted relatives, acquaintances and vendors stopping by the house constantly. In pre-independence Indonesia, the Toer home and the school where Pramoedya's father was principal were the loci for much of the town's nationalist activity; Pramoedya grew up in a world where conversation and storytelling were integral to daily life.

Pramoedya's parents were key influences in his life and works. His father's own resolve gave him the strength to survive sometimes long periods of incarceration as a political prisoner, first under the Dutch, then under the Sukarno and Suharto regimes.

His mother had a stronger impact on the writer's worldview; her bedtime tales filled him with the desire to create his own stories. She also inspired the many strong female characters in his works.

In the West, Pramoedya is best known for his longer prose, but in Indonesia, he is more highly respected as a writer of short stories. Whereas Western culture prizes the novel as the ultimate literary form, in Indonesia short stories and poetry have just as high a value – or higher. The orality of Indonesian culture may be why so many authors have preferred shorter literary works. In Indonesia, short stories and poems are meant to be read out loud, shared with friends and strangers just as parents share their family histories with their children.

This aspect of orality is highly evident in Pramoedya's work. One can easily imagine him reading these stories to his children, just as he described his own mother reading to him.

Willem Samuels

INDEPENDENCE DAY

Everywhere around the world, in the United States and Russia, all the more so in the newly founded nations – former Western colonies that were now in states of turbulence – and even in countries that had been the aggressors during the world war, the call for democracy had sounded. And like an echo repeating the sound of the voice in Kirno's own heart, there came to his ear the spirited cry of a political commentator on the radio, also shouting: *"Democracy!"*

Hearing the word, Kirno sighed, but because the human sigh so rarely achieves its purpose, he fell silent. Soon he sighed again. Carefully turning his neck, he looked around the room but could see nothing, only darkness, for he had surrendered his sight – not of his own volition, to be sure – to a Dutch bullet. The light in his eyes had faded, and now it was only his sense of hearing that sometimes convinced him he was still alive. But what of the bitterness he felt?

"Democracy," he whispered. Democracy is a beautiful thing and national independence a noble goal. About that, he agreed; but what rights did he now have in this free and democratic country? He didn't have the right to see. The suffering this caused him was real, and because it had so intimately entwined itself with his life, whenever he now thought of his own existence and interests, he derived a strange comfort from its presence. Because he could suffer, he knew he was alive.

Kirno smiled bitterly. When he tried to change his sitting position, the rubber tires of his wheelchair rubbed against their axles. He sighed yet again. When not lying prone in his bed, he was forced to sit in the wheelchair. He couldn't walk, not for a long time now. After the Dutch bullet had blinded him and he had fallen to the ground, a Dutch long-sword had severed both his legs from the trunk of his body.

"And I don't have the right to walk," he muttered, "not even a single metre."

Despite his own infirmity, Kirno felt himself more fortunate than other invalids. At least his parents were wealthy. They even owned a twelve-tube radio. After he had been brought down from the mountains to his hometown of Blora, he had discovered – even in the darkness that surrounded him – that the interests of his fellow townsmen had evolved. Now, with independence a fact of life, all people talked about were radios, cameras and bicycles. It appeared to him that he alone continued to focus his attention on democracy, the state of the nation and, naturally, his own miserable condition.

Like other suffering individuals, Kirno was unwilling to renounce what fond memories he still maintained, which is why he insisted on commemorating Independence Day. In the past, Independence Day had involved a rowdy and carefree communal celebration. And for independence, he had given his eyes and legs.

In years past, even pickpockets forgot to pick pockets on Independence Day, but now, with the newly established government having proved ineffectual in serving a starving country's needs, people had to think of their own exigencies; today the city's pickpockets would be out in force, lifting the wallets and handbags of both friend and stranger. But what could he do to fulfil his *own* needs, Kirno wondered. He couldn't see. He couldn't walk. All he could do now was sigh and listen to the radio's crackle and buzz.

Kirno took a deep breath, filling his lungs with

the cool morning air. The house was exceptionally still. He guessed that most of the household had gone to the city square to participate in the Independence Day celebrations that were being held there.

He beat his hands on the tray of his wheelchair and called for the manservant. Almost immediately, he heard the sound of footsteps, and assumed they were those of Mangun, who had joined his parents' household after Kirno had gone off to the mountains to fight.

"Yes, sir?" The voice was that of Mangun.

"Tune the radio to Jakarta." As the servant turned the knob to locate the right signal, Kirno listened to the radio's drone. "Did my mother go to the celebrations?" he asked.

"Yes, sir. She was asked to help welcome guests at the Regency."

"And my father?"

"He's there too."

"And Tini?"

"She left for school early. Said she was going to the parade."

Radio Jakarta began to broadcast light Western music.

"Is that really the Jakarta wavelength?"

The servant grunted in affirmation, then left.

Kirno listened to the music with a rising feeling of discontent. He turned his head around slowly, looking in every direction, as if expecting to see again – but everything was dark, completely black, without a sliver of light. One year. For a year now, he had been like this.

All at once the music playing on the radio died and was replaced by the booming sound of a mass rally, something Kirno suddenly realized he would never have the chance to see. Cries of *"Freedom!"* erupted from the throats of thousands of people.

Kirno lowered his head slowly, until his brow touched the tray of his wheelchair. He rested it there, listening to the distinctive voice of President Sukarno. But then, upon hearing a thunderous litany of slogans – *"For the people! For the nation! Liberty! Prosperity! Freedom! Democracy!"* – he lifted his head and drew a deep breath.

"The same thing! The same damn thing!" he cried out. "When is it going to change?"

An instant later, the servant was at Kirno's side, asking him in an apologetic tone: "What is it, sir? Did you call for something?"

Kirno mumbled, in a trembling voice: "The government has its income; the people have their own means. Everyone has his income and expenditures ..."

"I can't hear what you're saying," the servant said. "Is something wrong, sir?"

"No, nothing is wrong!" he barked. "Now go away." The servant turned away. "And turn off that radio before you go!"

Immediately, the sound of the radio died.

Kirno again lowered his forehead to the tray of his wheelchair and rested it there. Through his imagination passed images from the celebrations in Blora's central square. The square was filled with students in uniform and other spectators as well: farmers, civil servants on holiday, regular townspeople. Then there was the claque that always came to cheer on the day's orators, who screamed out their nationalist sentiments atop the raised podium. Flags were flying. People's clothes were dotted with perspiration from the midday heat. Ice cream sellers were making a windfall, probably more than on any other day of the year.

In Jakarta, Kirno imagined, the same scene was being played out in that city's Freedom Square, the only difference between Jakarta and Blora being that the former had a much larger pool of prey for pickpockets – and young men had much more freedom in finding partners.

Kirno moved his head from the tray of the wheelchair to the armrest, and then shouted an order to Mangun: "Find some gamelan music!"

The radio began to crackle again. Kirno caught snippets of Western songs, but no gamelan music.

"I can't find any, sir," the servant said in a tone of irritation, even as he continued to turn the radio knob.

Western music ... gamelan music ... or was it something else he wanted, Kirno asked himself. "Oh, what is it I want?" he moaned.

To his question, he heard the manservant reply: "I'm an old man, sir, and from what I've seen in this world, nobody ever knows exactly what he wants."

The kindness in the servant's voice drew from Kirno another question: "Why is it that I think everyone is mad?"

"You're living by yourself, is why," Mangun retorted. "You're keeping a distance from the world."

"Do you think that's what it is?"

"That's what my heart tells me," his servant

answered. "And my brain, too. When a man lives alone, he has only himself to listen to – and sometimes he ends up becoming his own teacher." As if having overstepped an invisible boundary between them, he added quickly: "I think I should go, sir. I've got work to do in the garden."

"Don't go," Kirno said. "I don't have anyone here to talk to." His tone of voice changed: "Tell me, Mangun, do you want to work as a servant forever?"

"I didn't choose my life, sir," the servant said, reflecting. "I've always had to accept what's come my way – even buffalo dung, if you'll forgive me for saying."

Kirno gurgled with understanding. "It sounds like you've had some bitter experiences." The tone of his voice indicated that he did not expect a reply. "I guess lots of people have to put up with bitter things in life ... You may go," he added finally, for his servant's benefit.

Upon hearing Mangun's receding footsteps,

Kirno's mind turned to the men he knew who had been crippled before he himself became an invalid. He knew men who had been blinded. He knew amputees. He also knew men who had lost their minds and wandered the streets, screaming about battles.

What happens to people such as those, who lacked the financial resources his own family had? *What about them*, Kirno asked himself. *What happens to them in this free and independent country of theirs?*

He provided his own answer: *They would resign themselves to their fates*. Resignation to one's fate, acceptance of one's destiny: these traits had once been seen as virtues in the days prior to independence. But what was their value now, in this modern world? Was it a virtue for a person to be resigned to eternal darkness? To living in a palace that cost a fortune to maintain?

Kirno banged his hand on the wheelchair tray.

Every muscle in his body tensed as he strove to control his mounting anger. Somewhere in the back of his mind, he heard a song coming off the radio. It was a new one – *Lili Marlene* – which he recalled having heard sung by a troop of Dutch soldiers as they rested after a jungle patrol. He listened to the song until it ended, until the last syllable had faded. Then he heard his own cry. Bowing his head, he heard the blast of the grenade he had thrown, and the rattle of his tommy gun as he had fired on the soldiers. Momentarily, he felt the same swell of victory in his chest that he had carried back to guerrilla headquarters.

These memories evaporated instantly when he heard someone calling his name from the doorway: "Kirno, *Mas* Kirno!"

Kirno turned his head toward the sound and forced himself to smile. "Is that you, Tini?"

He righted his position as his young sister walked into the room. He heard her light footsteps and then the cheerful sound of her voice: "I just came from the parade. It was great! We had a picnic at the school and we sang the national anthem and other songs, too."

He reached out for her. Finding her shoulder, he drew his sister closer to him and caressed her cheek with his hand. "Such a child you are!" he cooed. *One who knows nothing at all about the world,* he wanted to add, but said instead: "But there are lots of adults who are just as childish as you!"

He listened to his sister's giggles, but then felt her turn and run away. A moment later she was calling back to him: "It's Ati, Kirno! Ati is here!"

He tensed as he waited for the sound of a voice that once had aroused in him a gamut of emotions, not least love and desire. He listened as the woman he had wanted to marry spoke to his sister: "Tini, you're such a big girl now!"

He turned toward the voice, but of course he could see nothing. Although Kirno had come to accept this fact, his was a forced resignation. He couldn't imagine anyone willing to accept life as an invalid. He bowed his head again until it came to rest on the wheelchair tray, and turned his ear to pick up the voices in the hallway.

"Did you go to the parade, Tini?"

Why did her voice sound different? Kirno asked himself. A voice that had once excited his passions had, somehow, lost its special sound.

"I did!" Tini exclaimed. "I sang the national anthem and the proclamation song. And all of us kids got drinks and cakes."

"That must have been great fun!" Ati paused, then asked: "Where is your mother?"

"At the Regency. She's welcoming guests or something."

"And your father?"

"He's there, too."

"And Kirno? Where is he?"

"He's inside, but ..." Tini's voice fell to a near-whisper, making it more difficult for him to hear what she was saying. " ... but he can't walk. They cut off his legs."

"You mean his legs were amputated?" The shock was plain in the woman's voice.

"So now he has to use a wheelchair. When he wants to go somewhere, I always push him."

"I see ..." There was deep disappointment in that sound.

"And he's blind ..."

"Blind?"

To Kirno's ears, the question resembled a whimper. He lifted his head and slowly pulled himself erect. He leaned against the back of his wheelchair, waiting, with a furrowed brow.

"It's sad, isn't it?" That was Tini, speaking again.

He waited, but did not hear a reply. He thought of the freedom and the mobility he had once had, even in the days of colonialism, at a time when no one was shouting about democracy or liberty.

Then he heard the voice he had once adored: "Take me to him."

Kirno heard the light flip-flop of backless sandals, and the patter of a young girl's feet. He bowed his head quickly, lowering himself until it rested listlessly on the wheelchair tray. He heard his sister call his name, and then felt a woman's arms around him. He heard the sobbing of the young woman he used to love, before the Dutch had occupied Blora and he had fled to the jungle. He listened to her laboured breathing, then lifted his head and whispered: "Ati ... you've come at last."

"What happened, Kirno? Tell me what happened."

Suddenly gasping for breath, he could not answer until he had first calmed himself. Finally, he spoke in a slow, almost sonorous voice: "My friends are dead, Ati. They died and are now forgotten. And I might just as well be dead, for

I, too, have been forgotten. Now that the war is over, there's no time for people like me. Everyone is jockeying for power and positions within the country's new social structure."

Meeting with no argument, Kirno continued: "You're free to go anywhere now, Ati. You still possess that right. But me? I've lost all ordinary rights. Can you appreciate my situation, Ati? Can you understand how I feel, that I no longer have a place in the country I fought for?" He paused. "I'm not complaining, mind you. It's just that sometimes I get lonely, living like this, and sometimes – without meaning to – I have to let out the feelings inside my heart and mind." He paused again before asking: "Tell me, Ati, are you still as beautiful as you used to be?"

Now it was Ati who sighed.

"If you don't want to answer," Kirno said, "I can understand why. I can't hope for you to marry me. I wouldn't expect you to even consider it."

He heard an even deeper sigh before she finally began to speak: "Seeing you like this, Kirno ... I don't know what to think ... I don't know what to feel."

Kirno smiled. "Sometimes, Ati, a person can only begin to see things clearly after forgetting what he had once considered to be his future possibilities and thinking about realities. That is what all of us, too often, forget."

Neither said anything for a moment.

"Will you turn up the radio, please?" he asked Ati.

The sound of the radio filled the room: another Western song.

Kirno shook his head. "God, it's always the same thing. Don't they ever play anything else?"

Ati immediately attempted to find another station. Now, from the radio, came a fiery political speech.

"That's just as bad," Kirno complained. "Don't

people ever get tired of speeches?"

Ati seemed confused. "What are you asking?"

"That speech! It makes me feel like smashing the radio. It's nothing but nonsense."

She turned the knob again until she found a station playing gamelan music.

"That's it!" Kirno remarked. "I like to hear something soft and unhurried. I much prefer that to Western music."

"You've changed," Ati said.

"It's not that I wanted to change ... but what can I do now? Is there anything for me to hope for, anything for me to search for?"

"You never used to talk like that."

Kirno laughed. "Yes, but that was before, when I could hold you in my arms and kiss you when I wanted to. I thought I was strong; I thought a man was the master of his future." Kirno turned his head at the sound of his sister singing, which grew louder as she came nearer. "Tini," he said, "why don't you sing the *Butterfly* song for me? But switch off the radio first."

After switching off the radio, she sang the song her brother had requested. Kirno and Ati listened intently until it was finished.

"I used to be like you, Tini," Kirno said to her. At that remark, Tini suddenly began to cry. "Why are you crying?" her brother asked.

"Because I'm not like you," she whined. "I don't want to be crippled or blind."

Kirno tried to cheer her up: "Of course you don't, and you're not going to be! No one wants to be crippled or blind. I am ... but I'm not you. Please don't cry, Tini. I promise you, you're going to grow up to be a healthy and beautiful woman."

Tini stopped crying; now her muffled sobs filled the room's silence.

"Do you still want to sing?" Ati asked.

Tini shook her head. "I don't want to anymore." She sounded broken-hearted.

"Please," Ati begged. "Sing *The Elephant Song*! You must have learned that one at school."

Tini nodded and began to sing, although her sobbing was not fully under control. Her voice bridged the silence that lay between her brother and Ati. When the song was over, Ati gave Tini a kiss on the cheek.

"That was beautiful," Kirno remarked.

"It truly was," Ati added.

"I sang it in the singing competition," Tini explained.

"And did you get a prize?" Ati asked.

"Yes, I did – a slate board and chalk and a kiss on my cheek from the teacher."

"Your teacher must be very kind," Kirno commented.

"She really is," Tini exclaimed happily. Her tears had disappeared.

In the lull, they heard a noise outside – the voices of Kirno's parents – followed by the sound of footsteps coming into the house, and then a woman's voice: "Ati! Have you been here long?"

Ati moved away from Kirno to greet his parents. Kirno could make out only part of the ensuing conversation.

"... No, fate is not ours to choose," his mother was saying. "Just look what happened to Kirno ..." The she added: "You've not been around in such a long time ... Where have you been?"

"I was in the occupied territory most of the time."

"But you never sent word."

"How could I?" Ati asked.

"And now Kirno's a casualty ..."

Ati sighed. "The war claimed so many young men."

"He didn't lose only his sight and his mobility," Kirno's mother said.

"What do you mean?" Ati asked.

"You can't tell me that you're willing to marry

a cripple, Ati – even if he was crippled because of the war."

In the silence that followed this comment, Kirno felt Tini tugging on his shirt. He turned and put his arms around her, trying to fill the frightful emptiness he felt in both his and his sister's hearts. When their father began to speak, Tini put her hands on her brother's ears, but that did not prevent him from hearing.

"I prayed constantly, Ati. I prayed for God to watch over you and Kirno and for you to come safely through the war. Every night, we prayed. I know that in a battle, under a barrage of gunfire, no one can ever be truly safe ... but that didn't stop us both from staying up many a night, praying for Kirno's safety, and that he would someday get his wishes in life."

"It's true," Kirno's mother added, "we prayed as much as was possible for us to do."

Ati's voice sounded suddenly bitter. "Man

proposes, God disposes ..."

After a moment's silence, Kirno finally spoke up, unable to restrain his anger: "What are you talking about? I'm blind and crippled, and no amount of talk is going to change that!"

He could imagine his mother shaking her head sadly as she spoke: "I hope you can understand Kirno's attitude. He's angry and often loses his temper. It's only when Tini is around that he smiles and laughs."

"I do understand," Ati whispered.

"Tell me then, what do you think of Kirno now?"

Kirno spoke furiously: "What am I, Mother, a commodity to be weighed and judged in front of others?!"

Silence filled the room; no one dared to speak except Tini, who, without prompting, suddenly began to sing. The adults in the room listened to her clear and innocent voice. When the song was over, Kirno called for Ati to come closer.

"There's no point for you to discuss my life," he told her. "You know my situation now; you know my position in life. It's useless for you to talk about me." In a lighter tone, he then asked: "Where do you live now?"

"I live in Semarang," she replied.

"When did you arrive?"

"Just today, around noon." She paused before continuing: "You know my family, Kirno. You know I had no choice but to go with them to the occupied territory. After that, I couldn't contact you because you were in the area under guerrilla control."

"By that time," Kirno said, "I was in the home of the guerrilla chief. By the time you left, I had lost my eyes and legs." He swallowed before continuing: "You know, Ati, there's nothing more I would like than to be able to sit beside you forever and listen to your voice. But now it seems the only thing I can expect to have from you *is* your voice.

Only the sound of your voice tells me that you still exist." He took a deep breath. "That's it: your voice, and few memories. You must leave me, Ati ... Go home. That would be better for me."

Kirno listened as Ati turned and walked away, the sound of her footsteps growing fainter as she made her way to the door. His sister pattered behind. He heard indiscernible bits of conversation between the two of them, then the sound of his parents' voices – and then nothing at all. He lowered his head to the wheelchair tray and sat motionless. Around him was a darkness no light could illuminate.

Suddenly he heard the sound of several pairs of feet coming toward him, and then his mother's voice as she chastised him: "I say, Kirno, sometimes you can be so rude!" He didn't even attempt to move. "You drove Ati away the same way you'd chase off a stray cat."

Kirno felt Tini's arms encircle his neck. She

hugged him and whispered into his ear: "Ati was crying when she left."

"Don't you have any finer feelings, Kirno?" his mother asked.

Kirno immediately pulled himself erect. "And what good would they do me?" he asked hoarsely.

"Dear God," his mother moaned. "Ati comes to see you and you chase her away like there's nothing you need in the world, like you're the only person in the world! Don't you think she has feelings for you?"

"Shut up!" Kirno snarled. "What's the use of her feelings when all I can do is sit here in this wheelchair! Don't you get it, Mother? I'm going to be here for the rest of my life, until rheumatism, haemorrhoids and finally death come to call."

"You're so cold," his mother sighed.

Kirno snorted in reply.

Once again, Tini whispered in his ear: "Ati asked me if I could read, and when I told her I could, a little, she said I should read to you. I promised I would; but she wouldn't stop crying. Then she told me to always stay close to you, so that I could help you if you need anything."

Kirno exhaled through his lips.

"Is there anything you need now?" Tini asked.

Kirno smiled. "Maybe just another song."

Now Kirno's mother spoke up with a trembling voice: "That's all you ever want. Don't you have any feelings left? You punish your sister by ordering her to sing all the time, and chase away anyone who comes near you, only because they feel sorry for you. Then you snap at me and your father ..."

"Shut up and get out of here!" Kirno's voice was unforgiving.

His mother fled the room. After she had gone, Tini began to sing: *"On the seventeenth of August, of nineteen forty-five, independence was declared ..."*

Kirno hunched his body more and more, until his head was again resting on the tray of the wheelchair.

When the song was over, Kirno didn't move. Tini asked him: "Why are you being so quiet?" Upon hearing a stifled, barely audible sob, she embraced her brother again. She then chided him: "You asked me to sing that song, but you didn't even listen!" When he still didn't respond, she prompted: "Why are you crying, Kirno?"

Kirno continued to sob. He didn't raise his head. His body remained hunched. His eyes were hollow, completely empty; they could not catch even the smallest sliver of light. He could not see anything, except in his memory. He rustled, making the chair move slightly. It seemed to him that he had been sitting in that chair since time immemorial.

He heard Tini ask: "If you're blind, Kirno, what can you see?"

"Darkness," he told her, "nothing but darkness."

"You mean dark, like night?"

"As dark as night," Kirno confirmed. "And black as coal. Nothing but darkness."

"You can't see flowers?"

"No, Tini. All I can see is black, and nothing else."

"You mean *everything* is dark?"

"Yes, Tini, everything. That's why you're never going to be blind like me. You'll always be able to see Father and Mother and all your friends. And you're not going to be crippled, either. You'll always be able to walk and skip and jump."

When Tini didn't say anything, he suggested: "Why don't you tell me a story? Tell me about the singing competition at your school."

Tini immediately brightened. "Well, what happened is this: when the teacher asked if anyone could sing *On the Seventeenth of August*, I told her I could, but I didn't sing as good as Mini, so I lost. But when I sang *The Elephant Song* I won and the teacher gave me chalk and a slate board."

"That's wonderful, Tini! And what did you do after that?" Kirno asked.

Tini spoke with greater enthusiasm: "Then we went to the parade. First, we lined up outside school, and then, when we were all ready, we walked to the square. Almost all the students were there. It was really crowded. Everyone was waving flags. The band that was leading the parade never stopped playing. They played all these march songs that were really nice ...

"But it was very warm in the square. Everybody was hot. When people started cheering, we cheered, too. And then when people started shouting, we shouted too. That was a lot of fun! Then, when everyone clapped their hands, I started clapping too. They set off firecrackers –"

"I know," Kirno said, "I could hear them from here."

"Yeah, they were so loud I had to cover my ears. There were bits of paper everywhere. They fired the cannon, too, and when that exploded I almost screamed because I was so scared. There was a lot of smoke. And after that, the band played again, and we sang the national anthem. I like that song. I liked the way they played. The way they play it on the radio isn't nearly as good."

Kirno suddenly felt a yearning for something he could not define. He coughed and cleared his throat. Was it Ati he longed for? He shook his head weakly. His sight? He shook his head again. His legs? No. He didn't know. All he knew was that he felt incredibly lonely. He suddenly threw out his arms to embrace his sister. He stroked her hair and spoke to her lovingly. "You're such a sweet girl, Tini. Do you think you'd like to sing for me?"

Tini laughed and wiggled from her brother's embrace. "It's *your* turn to sing for *me!*" she declared. "Why don't you sing *On the Seventeenth of August*."

Kirno took a deep breath and began to sing, slowly and with resonance in his voice. While singing, he saw himself as he once was, marching, standing tall and with pride in the city of Pati on Independence Day. A full battalion of men had participated that day; though dressed haphazardly, they were fully armed. But now that drama was over. He tried to picture Independence Day at the guerrilla camp, but couldn't retrieve any images at all from memory. By that time he had lost his sight, and had only been able to tell what was happening from the voices around him. Voices: that was all he could remember.

Kirno's singing had become a moan. Finally, with tears trickling down his cheeks, he stopped. He kissed his sister, who responded with a hug.

"Why are you crying, Kirno?"

"I'm crying because I can't celebrate Independence Day the way you do, Tini. I used to love to watch our troops marching in parade, but now I can't." His voice suddenly sounded harsh, even to his own ear: "I can't do anything, I don't *want* to do anything, I don't need anything anymore – not the Seventeenth of August, not a thousand

Independence Days." Then he said, beneath his breath: "All I want is death."

Tini attempted to divert her brother's sadness: "Sing something else, Kirno. Why don't you sing *The Elephant Song*?"

After swallowing hard, Kirno rose in song again: a simple, traditional tune that reminded him of Ati – the woman he loved, the same woman he had driven away earlier that day. He could hear, faintly, the voice of this woman he had once adored. But marriage to her now was impossible. She deserved a man who would not bring shame or disgrace on her or her family.

He paused in his song to catch his breath and found himself crying anew. He hastily wiped his tears and then hugged and kissed his sister again.

"I want you to do me a favour," he whispered. "Call Mother in here for me, will you?"

Kirno listened to Tini's footsteps as she left the room. Moments later, he heard a different set of footsteps approach.

"Do you want something, Kirno?" his mother asked.

"I want to go away from here," he told her.

"In the condition you're in? How could you?" Kirno's mother shook her head. "You certainly gave us some trouble today."

"I know, Mother," Kirno admitted, "but I don't do it on purpose. I just don't want to have to be taken care of. That's why it would be best if I left. I don't want to give you any more trouble."

All he heard in reply was a long sigh.

"I should go to a home for invalids. I'd be mixing with people of my own kind. I might even be happy living there. And you won't have to trouble yourself with me, or put up with my temper. I'm not happy here – you know that – and I'm sorry that I was brought back here in the first place."

Not hearing his mother attempt to stop him from speaking further, he continued: "And besides, I don't want to poison Tini with this suffering of mine."

"I know that you're not happy, Kirno," his mother said softly, "but I don't want you to go. I don't want anyone else taking care of you."

"But can't you see," he argued, "part of my unhappiness is due to all the restrictions you place on me here. I can't do this, I can't do that ..." He stopped and took a deep breath, trying to steady his voice. "I was so happy before this happened. I could go anywhere I wanted, do what I wanted to do. Did you ever forbid me then? No – because you didn't have the right to. I'd be happy if I weren't a cripple. I'd be happy if I hadn't taken up arms. I'd probably be happy if I had followed Father's example: when the nationalists were in power, he stood behind them; when the Reds got the upper hand, he gave his support to them; when the Dutch came back, he worked with them; and, finally, when the

Republic was formed, he became a republican."

"You're speaking badly of your father."

Kirno detected guilt in his mother's voice. "But isn't it true?" he asked.

She did not reply, and in the silence that followed, the indefinable longing he had felt earlier returned.

"It would be better for me to go away from here," he stated again.

"But where would you go, Kirno?" Now it was Tini speaking, her voice anxious.

"I'd go to a place where there are other people like me."

"But *where*, Kirno?"

"There are homes for disabled people," he told her.

Tini began to cry. "No, Kirno, you can't. Ati told me that I should take care of you. And she asked me to read to you. I can't do that if you go away."

Not knowing what to say, Kirno remained silent.

"She told me that she's not going to come back here anymore because you don't want her here. She said that she was going back to Semarang. But if she changes her mind and comes back, and you're not here, and if she asks me if I've been reading to you, what am I going to tell her?"

Kirno put his arms around Tini and kissed her. His voice trembled as he spoke: "You have lots of friends, Tini; you should be playing with them. You don't have to sing for me or read for me. You should be playing with your own friends."

Kirno felt her body begin to shake, and then he, too, began to cry.

"You mustn't cry," he whispered. "You should be out playing with your friends. I don't have any friends here."

"But I'm here!" Tini wailed.

"But when you go to school, or somewhere else, I don't have any."

"That's enough, Kirno," his mother interjected.

"What will you think of next? This is your home. This is where you live."

"This is not my home," Kirno insisted.

"Where is it, then?"

"In an invalid ward, that's where!" he said. He spoke more softly to his sister: "In the morning you have to go to school, Tini, and in the afternoon you must play with your friends."

"But you can't go away, Kirno. You can't."

"I'll come back ... and when I come back, I won't be blind anymore, and I'll be able to walk. When I come back, you'll have a fit and healthy brother. We'll go to the city square together. Won't you like that, Tini? And on Independence Day, we'll go to the celebration together. We'll walk amongst the crowd and watch the horse race ... You'd like that, wouldn't you?"

"Yes, I would," Tini answered.

"Then I can go, can't I?" Hearing no reply, Kirno raised his voice: "Ask someone to take me to the home for invalids. Right now! This is Hell here. I hate this place, and I hate living here."

His voice was never again heard in his family home. Never again did he and his sister sing together. Thereafter, Kirno's parents were able to live in peace, without being obliged to care for their blind, disabled son.

At first, Tini asked them when Kirno was coming back.

Later, she never asked at all.

INEM

Amongst the girls I knew, Inem was my best friend. She was eight – just two years older than me – and much like the other girls I knew. If there was anything that distinguished her, it was that she was considerably prettier than the other girls in my neighbourhood. She lived at my parents' home, where her family had placed her. In return for room and board, she helped in the kitchen and looked after my younger siblings and me.

In addition to being pretty, Inem was also polite, clever and hardworking – not pampered at all. These traits helped to spread her good name to adjoining neighbourhoods. She would make a fine daughter-in-law someday, it was said. And sure enough, one day, when Inem was boiling drinking water in the kitchen, she announced to me: "I'm going to be married!"

"No, you're not!" I told her.

"I am, I really am. The proposal came a week ago. My parents and all my other relatives think it's a good idea."

"Wow! That'll be fun!" I shouted ecstatically.

"It sure will," she agreed. "They'll buy me all these beautiful new clothes. And I'll get to wear a bridal dress and have flowers in my hair and powder, mascara and eyeshadow. I'm going to like that!"

Inem was telling the truth, as we were soon to learn when, one evening, not long afterward, Inem's mother called on mine.

Inem's mother earned what money she could from making batik. That's what the women in the area did when they weren't working in the rice fields. Some made batik wraparound *kain*; others made headcloths. The poorer women, like Inem's mother, worked on headcloths. Not only did it take less time to make one, they received payment for their work much sooner. On average, a woman could make between eight and eleven headcloths a day. Toko Ijo, the store that bought the headcloths that Inem's mother made, supplied her with cotton fabric and wax. For every two headcloths that she produced, she was paid one and a half Dutch cents.

Inem's father, on the other hand, liked to gamble – with gamecocks, especially. All day, every day, he spent cockfighting. When his rooster lost, he had to turn it over to the victor's owner, plus pay the owner two and a half *rupiah*, or – at the very least – seventy-five Dutch cents. And when he wasn't doing this, he was playing cards with his neighbours for an ante of one cent per hand.

Sometimes Inem's father would go off on foot and not come back for a month or more. Generally, his return home meant that he had somehow managed to make some money. My mother once told me that his real source of income came from robbing travellers on the road that ran through the huge teakwood plantation that lay between Blora, our hometown, and the coastal town of Rembang. I was in first grade at the time, and heard lots of stories about robbers, bandits, killers and thieves. Because of them, and because of what my mother told me, I came to be terrified of Inem's father.

Everyone knew Inem's father was a thief, but no one dared to report him to the police. And anyway, no one could prove that he was a thief, and he was never arrested. Besides, it seemed like almost all of Inem's mother's male relatives were policemen. One was even a top detective. Even Inem's father had once been a policeman, but had lost his job on account of taking bribes.

Mother also told me that Inem's father had been a thief even before becoming a policeman. The government, as a means of containing crime in the area, had made him a policeman and had sicced him on his former associates. After that, he'd quit robbing people, she said, but that didn't stop her or others from viewing him with suspicion.

The day Inem's mother came calling, Inem was in the kitchen, heating water. When Mother went to greet her visitor, I tagged along, even when they convened in the sitting room, where they arranged themselves on a low, red-coloured wooden daybed.

It was Inem's mother who opened the conversation: "Ma'am, I've come to ask to take Inem home," she said.

"But why? Isn't it better for her here?" my mother enquired. "You don't have to pay anything for her to stay here, and she's learning how to cook."

"I know that, Ma'am, but I plan for her to get married after the harvest is in."

"Married?!" My mother was shocked.

"Yes, Ma'am. She's old enough – all of eight now," Inem's mother said in affirmation.

At this, my mother laughed – a reaction that excited in our visitor a look of surprise.

"Eight years old? Isn't that a bit too young?" my mother asked.

"We're not rich people, Ma'am, and the way I see it, she's already a year too old. Asih, you know, she had her daughter married off when she was two years younger."

Mother tried to dissuade her, but Inem's mother wouldn't hear of it: "I just feel lucky someone's proposed," she argued, "and if we let this proposal go by, there might not be another one. Imagine the shame of having a daughter become an old maid! Besides, once she's married, she might even be able to help lighten the load around the house."

Mother let this pass, but gave me a nudge. "Go get the betel set and spittoon."

I did as ordered, fetching the brass spittoon and the decorative box that contained all the ingredients for chewing betel.

"And your man, what does he have to say about this?"

"Oh, Inem's father agrees," the woman said, "especially as Markaban – that's the name of the boy who's proposing – is the son of a rich man, and an only child, too. He's already begun to help his father, trading cattle in Rembang, Cepu, Medang, Pati, Ngawen and here in Blora, too."

This information seemed to cheer Mother, though I could not understand why. She then called for Inem, who was still at work in the kitchen.

When Inem came into the room, Mother asked her: "Inem, do you want to get married?"

Inem bowed her head; she held my mother in great respect, and always deferred to her. I noticed that Inem was smiling radiantly, but she often looked like that: if you gave Inem something that made her happy, she would always respond with a huge smile. *Thank you* was not something she was used to saying. Amongst the people in our area, simple folk by and large, the expression 'thank you' was an unfamiliar phrase. A beaming smile, a happy look on one's face: this was the way gratitude was expressed.

"Yes, Ma'am," Inem finally whispered, almost inaudibly.

My mother and Inem's mother each prepared a cud of betel. Mother rarely chewed betel, doing so only when she had a woman visitor. Every few moments, the silence in the room was broken by the twang of their spitting into the brass spittoon.

After Inem had returned to the kitchen, Mother stated flatly: "It's not right for children to marry."

Inem's mother raised her eyebrows, but didn't respond. I saw no curiosity in her eyes, merely a hint of surprise.

"I was eighteen when I got married," Mother said. The look on Inem's mother's face vanished. Her unspoken question had been answered. But still, she didn't say anything. "It's not right for children to marry," Mother repeated.

Once again, Inem's mother stared, as if not

knowing what to say.

"Their children will be stunted," Mother added.

Again, the look of puzzlement on Inem's mother face faded. "I'm sure you're right, Ma'am ..." Then she said, evenly: "My mother was eight when she got married."

As if she had not heard what her guest said, Mother continued: "Not only will they be stunted, their health will be poorly affected."

"I'm sure you're right, Ma'am, but my own family is long-lived. My mother is still alive, and she's at least fifty-nine. My grandmother is living, too. She must be about seventy-four. And she's still strong – strong enough to pound corn, anyway."

Still ignoring her, Mother added: "... Especially if the husband is young, too."

"Of course, Ma'am, but Markaban is seventeen."

"Seventeen! My husband was *thirty* when he married me."

Inem's mother said nothing. She kept moving

the betel cud around between her upper and lower lips and teeth. One moment the wad would be on the right side of her mouth, the next moment on the left. Then she would roll the cud tightly in her fingers and use it to scrub her blackened teeth.

Mother had no more arguments with which to dissuade her guest's intention.

"Well, if you've made up your mind to marry Inem off, I can only hope that she'll get a husband who takes good care of her. I just hope that he's the right man for her, the one destined to be her mate."

Inem's mother then left the house, still churning the cud of tobacco around inside her mouth.

After she had gone Mother said softly to me: "I hope nothing bad comes to that child."

"Why would anything bad happen?" I asked her.

"Never mind, don't pay attention to me," she said, before changing the subject. "At least, if her family's situation improves, we might stop losing our chickens."

"Is *that* who's stealing our chickens?"

"Never mind," she repeated, and then spoke slowly, as if to herself: "And just a child! Eight years old. Such a shame. But they need money, I suppose, and the only way to get it is by marrying off their daughter."

Thereafter, Mother left the house and went to the garden out back, where she gathered some string beans for our dinner.

Fifteen days after her visit, Inem's mother came to the house again, this time to take away Inem for good. She seemed extremely relieved when Inem did not object. When Inem was ready to go – to leave me and her foster family forever – she came to look for me at the kitchen door.

"Goodbye," she said. "I'm going home now." She said this very softly; but she always spoke softly. In my small town, this was one way of showing respect. And then she left, as cheerful as any young girl expecting to receive a new dress.

After Inem stopped living at our house, I felt the loss of my close friend very deeply. From then on, it wasn't Inem who took me to the bathroom at night to wash my feet before going to bed, but an older foster sister.

At times I could hardly contain my longing to see Inem. Often, when lying in bed, I would recall the image of Inem's mother taking her daughter by the hand, leading her out of the house and escorting her to their own house, which was located behind ours, separated from our property only by a wooden fence.

During the first month after Inem's departure, I often went to her house to play, but whenever Mother found out where I had been, she'd become angry with me. "What's the use of going there?" she'd ask. "You're not going to learn anything in that house."

What could I say? I had no answer. Whenever Mother scolded me, she had her reasons, and her words of reprimand were a wall that none of my excuses could ever scale. My best recourse was to say nothing at all.

But then when I said nothing, she was sure to continue: "What's the point of playing with Inem? Aren't there lots of other children you can play with? Inem is a woman now, and is going to be married soon."

Despite my mother's objections, I continued to sneak over to Inem's house. I found some of my mother's prohibitions surprising; it was as if their only reason for existence was to be violated. And in violating them, I have to admit, I derived a certain pleasure. For children such as I was, at that time and in that place, there were a startling number of rules and taboos. It seemed as if the whole world was watching us children, conspiring to keep us from doing anything we wanted to do. There was almost no getting around the perception that this world was meant only for adults.

For five days before Inem's wedding, her family

prepared food and special cakes. As a result, I spent more time than ever at her house.

The day before the wedding, Inem's bridal preparations began. Mother sent me to her house with five kilograms of rice and twenty-five cents as a contribution to the event. That evening, after Inem was prepared, all the children in the neighbourhood gathered at her place to stare at her in admiration.

Inem's eyebrows and the fine hairs on her forehead and temples had been trimmed and shaped with a razor, their lines accentuated by liner and mascara. Her hair had been thickened and made longer with a switch, then ratted and shaped into a high chignon. Sprouting from this was a spray of tiny paper flowers, the stems of which were made of fine, tightly wound springs that swayed with the movement of the bride's head. Inem's *kebaya*, the hip-length buttoned blouse, was satin, and her *kain* was an expensive length of batik from Solo. Inem's family had obtained these things from a rental shop in the Chinese district near the town square. Her gold rings and bracelets were rented, too.

The house was festooned with banyan cuttings and coconut fronds. Tricoloured bunting, red, white and blue – cinched at regular intervals to create a series of upside-down fans – ran around the corners of the room. The house pillars, too, had been wrapped with tricoloured ribbon.

Mother herself went over to help with the preparations, though not for very long; in less than an hour she was back home. She rarely did this sort of thing, except for our closest neighbours.

At that same time, a cartload of gifts from Inem's husband-to-be arrived at Inem's home: a big basket of cakes, a billy goat, a large sack of rice, a bag of salt, a gunny sack of husked coconut and a half-sack of sugar.

As the wedding feast was being held just after the harvest, rice was cheap – and when rice is cheap, all other foodstuffs are cheap, too, which is why the post-harvest period is the most favoured time for weddings. It was also why Inem's family was unable to hold a *wayang kulit* performance: all the puppeteers in the area had already been contracted by other families or communities.

Wayang kulit – shadow-puppet theatre – was the most popular form of local entertainment. There were three kinds of *wayang* in our area: the classical *wayang purwa* shadow theatre, which recounted stories from the Javanese version of the *Mahabharata* and *Ramayana* epics and other related legends; the flat, wooden *wayang krucil* puppets, generally used to enact stories of foreign or historical origin from Arabia, Persia, India, China and the ancient Majapahit era; and the three-dimensional *wayang golek* puppets – but these wooden doll-puppets were not especially popular in our region.

Because no puppeteers were available, Inem's family decided to hire a female dance troupe. At first, this caused some contention: it was well known that Inem's mother's side of the family was devout. On this point, however, Inem's father would not back down, and in the end, a dance troupe arrived, complete with a gamelan orchestra and female *tayuban* dancers.

In our area, a *tayuban* performance was generally reserved for adult males, who participated in the dance along with young children whose knowledge of sexual matters did not extend much beyond kissing, and who were there only to watch. Pubescent boys generally shunned *tayuban* performances because they usually ended up being embarrassed by the female dancers.

No woman of respect would ever attend. In order to arouse excitement amongst the largely male audience, a *tayuban* performance was always accompanied by the consumption of alcoholic beverages – palm wine, beer, whiskey or gin.

The *tayuban* for Inem's wedding went on, intermittently, for two days and nights. We children had a great time of it, watching the men and women dancing and kissing, clinking their glasses together and gulping down shot after shot of liquor as they danced and sang. Although Mother forbade me to watch, I went on the sly.

"Why do you insist on going over there? Sinners, is what they are. Just look at your religion teacher. Is he there? No, he's not. You must have noticed that. And he is Inem's uncle!"

Inem's uncle, my religion teacher, also lived behind our house – just to the right of Inem's. His absence at the *tayuban* performance was widely noted. The commentary on everyone's tongue was that Inem's uncle was a pious man, and her father an incorrigible reprobate.

My mother justified her anger with an argument I did not, at that time, comprehend: "Those people have no respect for women. Are you aware of that?" she asked incisively.

When the bridegroom came to the house to be

formally introduced to his bride, Inem, who had been seated on the wedding dais, was led forth from her home. At the door to the veranda, where the bridegroom now waited, she knelt before her husband-to-be and demonstrated her obeisance to him by washing his feet with flower water from a brass vase. The couple were then bound and together conducted to the dais.

The guests repeated, mantra-like: *One child becomes two. One child becomes two. One child becomes two ...* The women's faces glowed as if they themselves were the recipients of happiness to come.

It was then I noticed that Inem was crying. Her tears had smudged her makeup and left watermarks in the powder as they trickled down her face.

Later, at home, when I asked my mother why Inem had been crying, she told me: "When a bride cries, it's because she is thinking of her departed ancestors. Their spirits are at the ceremony, and they are happy because their descendant has been safely married."

I didn't give much thought to her reply, but later, I found out that Inem had been crying because she had to urinate, but was afraid to tell anyone.

The wedding celebration ended uneventfully, and Inem's home returned to its usual state. No more guests appeared with contributions. Now, instead, it was the money collectors who began to call. By this time, however, Inem's father had left town on one of his travels.

After the wedding, Inem and her mother spent their days and nights making batik headcloths. If one were to pass by their home at three o'clock in the morning, there would be a good chance of finding them still working, with smoke rising from the pot of heated wax between them.

Often, the sound of raised voices could also be heard emanating from the house. Once, when I was sleeping with Mother in her bed, a loud scream awakened me: *"No! I don't want to!"*

Later that same night, I heard the scream repeated again and again, in time with a thud-like sound and then pounding on a door. I knew it was Inem screaming; I recognized her voice.

"Why is Inem screaming?" I asked my mother.

"They're fighting. I just hope nothing bad happens to that little girl," she added, without further explanation.

I persisted with my questions: "Why should anything bad happen to her?"

Mother wouldn't answer me. Finally, after the screaming and shouting had subsided, we fell asleep again. But the next night – and almost every other night that followed – we heard those screams again. Screaming, screaming ... incessant screaming. And every time I heard it, I asked my mother what it meant, but she would never give me a satisfactory answer. At best, she might sigh: 'Such a pity ... such a poor little thing ..."

One day, Inem appeared at the door to our house and went to find my mother straight away. Inem's face was pale and ashen, and even before she tried to speak, she began to cry – though in a soft and respectful way.

"Why are you crying, Inem?" Mother asked her. "Have you been fighting again?"

Inem stuttered between her sobs: "Please take me back, Ma'am. I hope you'll take me back."

"But you have a husband now, don't you, Inem?"

Inem began to cry again. "I can't take it, Ma'am," she said through her tears.

"But why, Inem? Don't you like your husband?"

"Please, Ma'am. Take pity on me. Every night, all he does is wrestle with me and try to get on top of me."

"But can't you say to him, 'Please don't do that, dear'?"

"I'm afraid, Ma'am. I'm afraid of him. He's so big, and when he starts to squeeze me he hugs me so tight I can't even breathe. Won't you please take me back, Ma'am?" she pleaded.

"If you didn't have a husband, Inem, of course I'd take you back. But you're married now ..."

Hearing my mother's answer, Inem began to cry that much harder. "But I don't want a husband, Ma'am!"

"You might not want one, but you have one, Inem. Maybe, in time, your husband will change for the better, and the two of you will be happy. You wanted to get married, didn't you?"

"Yes, Ma'am, but ... but ..."

"There are no 'buts' about it. No matter what, a woman must serve her husband faithfully," Mother advised. "If you can't do that, Inem, your ancestors will look down and curse you."

Inem was now crying so hard that she could no longer speak. My mother continued: "I want you to promise me, Inem, that you will always prepare your husband's meals, and that when your work is finished, you will pray that God watches over him and keeps him safe. You must promise to wash his clothes, and you must massage him when he comes home tired from work. You must take care of him if ever he falls ill."

Inem said nothing as tears streamed down her face.

"Go home, Inem, and from now on, serve your husband faithfully. No matter if he's good or bad, you must serve him faithfully. He is your husband, after all."

Inem, who was sitting weakly on the floor, did not stir.

"Now stand up, and go home to your husband. If you ... If you were to leave him, the consequences would not be good for you, either now or in the future."

Head bowed, Inem answered submissively: "Yes, Ma'am." Then she picked herself up slowly and made her way home.

"How sad, she's so young," Mother said, after she had gone.

"Mother ... Does Father ever wrestle with you?" I asked.

Mother searched my eyes carefully. Her scrutiny then vanished, and she smiled.

"No," she said. "Your father is the best person in the whole world." She went to the kitchen and returned with a hoe to work with me in the garden.

A year passed by, unnoticed. And then, one day, Inem came to the house again. She had grown in that time, and now looked almost like an adult – though she was barely nine. As in the past, she went directly to Mother. When she found her, she sat, head bowed, on the floor before her.

"Ma'am, I don't have a husband anymore," she announced.

"What's that you said, Inem?"

"I don't have a husband now."

"You're divorced?" my mother asked.

"Yes, Ma'am."

"But why?" Inem said nothing. "Didn't you serve him faithfully?"

"I think I was a good wife to him, Ma'am."

"But did you massage him when he came home tired from work?" Mother probed.

"Yes, Ma'am, I did everything you told me to."

"Then why did he divorce you?"

"He beat me," she stated, "all the time."

"He beat you? A young girl like you?"

"I think I did everything to be a good wife, Ma'am. But letting him beat me, Ma'am, and putting up with the pain, is that part of being a good wife, Ma'am?" She asked this in true consternation.

Mother said nothing as she studied Inem's eyes. "He beat you ..." she whispered, as if to herself.

"Yes, Ma'am, he beat me – just like my parents do."

"Maybe you didn't serve him faithfully enough. A husband would never beat his wife if she's been truly good to him."

Inem said nothing to this. Instead, she asked: "Will you take me back, Ma'am?"

My mother answered without hesitation: "Inem, you're a divorced woman and there are grown boys here in this house. That wouldn't look right to people, would it now?"

"But they wouldn't beat me," she answered simply.

"That's not what I meant, Inem. For a divorced woman as young as you to be in a place where there are lots of men around just wouldn't look right."

"Is there something wrong with me, Ma'am?"

"No, Inem, it's a question of propriety."

"I don't know what that means, Ma'am. Are you saying that's why I can't stay here?"

"Yes, Inem, that is what I'm saying."

Inem was left without another word to say. She remained seated on the floor, as if she had no intention of leaving.

Mother bowed and patted Inem's shoulder

consolingly. "I think the best thing for you to do would be to help your parents earn a living. I'm truly sorry that I can't take you back."

Teardrops appeared in the corners of the child-woman's eyes. Finally, Inem stood. Picking up her feet listlessly, she left our house to return to her parents' home. From that time onward, she was seldom seen anymore.

Thereafter, this nine-year-old divorcée – for being nothing but a burden on her family's household – could be beaten by anyone at will: by her mother, her brothers, her uncles, her neighbours, her aunts. But she never again came to our house. I'd often hear her cries of pain, and when she screamed, I'd cover my ears with my hands.

Meanwhile, Mother continued to uphold propriety and the family's good name.

CIRCUMCISION

Like other village children, I spent my evenings at the local prayer house learning to recite the Qur'an. Nothing could have pleased us more than to be there. For recitation lessons, we paid two and a half Dutch cents per week, which was used to buy oil for the lamps. Lessons began at five-thirty in the evening and continued until nine; they were the one and only excuse we had for getting out of doing our homework.

What I'm calling 'recitation lessons' actually consisted of nothing more than telling jokes, talking in fevered whispers about sex and annoying the devotees who had come to say their sunset or evening prayers while we waited for our own turn to be called. This was my world at the age of nine.

Like my friends, I wanted to be a good Muslim, though few of us, at our age, had been circumcised. But then one of my friends did get circumcised, and a large celebration was held for him. This is when I began to wonder: *If I haven't been circumcised, am I really a Muslim?* I mulled over this question, but didn't let anyone know what I was thinking.

In my small hometown of Blora, boys were usually circumcised between the ages of eight and thirteen, generally in as grand a style as family circumstances permitted. Girls underwent symbolic circumcision at the age of fifteen days, without any kind of celebration.

One night, my father came home and talked to me about circumcision. I had no idea where he had been, but he was in a very buoyant mood. The house was dark; all the lamps had been extinguished except for one, in the central hall where I was sitting with my mother, listening to her tell me a story about an old man who kept on getting married – a pious man, presumably, as he had been to Makkah and was called *haji* to indicate that he had made the pilgrimage to Islam's holiest seat. The story was a good one, but because of my father's sudden return, it died then and there.

"Do you think you're brave enough to be circumcised?" he asked me, a hopeful smile on his lips.

I didn't know what to say. I wanted to be a good Muslim, but my father's surprise offer terrified me. Then again, my father always terrified me. But for some reason, his smile that night made all my fears disappear.

"Yes, I am!" I told him.

His smile broadened and he laughed congenially. "What would you like to wear for your circumcision, a wraparound batik *kain* or a tube *sarung*?"

"A *kain*," I answered.

He then turned to my seven-year old brother, who was also in the room. "And what about you, Tato? Are you brave enough, too?"

Tato laughed happily: "Sure I am!"

Father, too, laughed contentedly. The light from the lamp illuminated his even, white teeth and pink gums.

Mother rose from the mat she had rolled out on the floor earlier, before starting her bedtime story.

"When do you want to have them circumcised?" she asked.

"As soon as possible," my father replied.

He then rose from his chair and walked away, into the darkness of the house, to his bedroom.

Mother stretched out on the mat again but did not continue her story about the marriage-happy *haji*. Instead, she looked at us: "You boys must give thanks to God that your father is going to have you both circumcised."

"We will, Mother," we answered in unison.

"Your dear departed grandmother and all your other ancestors in Heaven will be very pleased to know that you have been circumcised."

"Yes, Mother," we said again.

That night I could scarcely sleep as I thought of how much the circumcision would hurt. But then I also began to think of the new *kain* and the new pair of sandals I would likely receive – along with all the other new clothes, and a headcloth and prayer mat as well. On top of that, I wouldn't have to go to school, and there would be numerous guests. I was almost sure to receive lots of gifts.

I imagined the happiness I would feel from owning my own *kain* and headcloth, for these items were not only signs of being a good Muslim – they were signs of being a good Javanese as well, something I also wanted to be. I was also sure to be given at least one *sarung*, maybe two or even three. My uncircumcised friends would be jealous; that thought, too, gave me a thrill.

The following morning, I rose from my bed full of excitement. Tato and I set off for school with plenty of time to spare. Usually, our legs balked at walking to school, but that day they flew. All our classmates soon heard the news, and the boys who weren't circumcised – especially the older ones – looked at us with newfound respect. Even the teachers cast a kindly gaze on us, for soon we were going to be *bona fide*, circumcised Muslims.

And when that happened – and this was the most important thing of all – we would have the right to a place in Heaven. We'd no longer have to wish for the many beautiful things we'd always hoped for, but which we had never been able to obtain, for they would be ours.

At the prayer house, the news also created a sensation amongst my friends, and our religion teacher gave me the same kindly look that my teachers at school had displayed. I suddenly felt taller, more important than my friends. I could see, very clearly, Heaven's gates standing wide open for me. And sure enough, just as our religion teacher had also promised, there they were: the beautiful *houris*, young maidens waiting to tend to my needs. Each one was as beautiful as a certain girl at my school that all the boys talked about.

"After I'm circumcised, I'll be a true Muslim," I told the *kiai*. "I'll have the right to go to Heaven!"

The man laughed cheerfully. "And you'll have forty-four *houris* to wait on you!"

"But I don't want any that have six or eight breasts, like a dog," I told him. "I want them to look like Sriati, my classmate at school. She's beautiful."

The *kiai* laughed again.

"And I'll go fishing in rivers of milk every day," Tato chimed in.

Our teacher's mouth opened wider with laughter, baring a disgusting set of teeth that looked like they'd never been brushed.

Our older and uncircumcised friends listened to this conversation silently. I could see fear in their eyes: the fear of missing out on their share of *houris*, and the fear of going not to Heaven but to Hell.

Starting that evening, we followed our recitation lessons diligently, and made sure to finish our homework in short order, too. We also fasted from Monday to Thursday every week until the end of the school year. As a result of this extra labour, I passed to the next grade easily.

Two weeks before the end of the school year, my father, the principal of our school, decided to stage a play with the children as actors. Our circumcision ceremony would be held the following day. Father had decided, then and there, to make this an annual event. That way, the poorer boys in school, whose parents could not afford to hold separate celebrations, would have the chance to be circumcised as well.

At this – my father's first attempt at starting a new tradition – the response of the townspeople was not what he had expected. Many parents with sons of circumcision age were apparently embarrassed to have someone else pay for their sons' circumcision ceremonies. In the end, there were only six boys to be circumcised: my brother Tato and me; a ten-year-old cousin of ours; a sixteen-year-old foster brother; and two boys from poor families who lived outside of town. Another foster brother, who was eighteen and had already had a child with our servant, refused to participate. He insisted that his own father would arrange a ceremony for him.

That year, I was in the sixth grade and Tato was in

the second. Both of us passed. Five days before the celebration, the boys who were to be circumcised were made to memorize a *panembrama*, a Javanese welcome song. On the night of the play, we were to appear onstage and announce to the audience – in song – that we were to be circumcised the next day; we were also to request that they offer their prayers for a successful event.

One of our teachers wrote a play about a lost goat, in which all the roles were played by the male students.

Finally, the long-awaited day arrived. The previous evening, our grandmother had given Tato and me green silk *sarungs*. Our mother gave us lacquered wooden sandals and blue shirts. The girls in school gave us switches for keeping flies away during the ceremony, and our father gave us eight Dutch-language children's books. All these gifts made us forget about the pain we were to feel the following day.

On the night of the play, the school was packed

with spectators. Food was served: sweet potatoes and boiled peanuts; fermented cassava; *gemblong* made of sweetened sticky rice; and other snacks. Before the performance was to begin, the six of us who were to be circumcised were made to line up onstage. I was outfitted in a *kain* and headcloth, as was Tato. The other boys were bareheaded. The curtain opened, and the gamelan orchestra began to play. We bowed in respect to the audience. I felt so incredibly proud of myself at that moment. All eyes were focused on us as we sang out that the following day we were to be circumcised. The girls looked at us with awe; there would soon be six more eligible men in town.

After our song, the audience applauded loudly, and we took another bow. The curtain was then closed, and we were relieved of further responsibility.

In my hometown, there was very little public entertainment – which is why, I suppose, people came from all parts of the city to watch our performance of *The Lost Goat*. The school's large central classroom, which was usually subdivided into four sections during the regular school day, had been transformed into a single hall that was now filled with people.

The musical entertainment that night varied greatly; besides the gamelan orchestral works, there were new popular songs such as *Peanut Flower* and *Rose Mary*, cowboy songs, theatrical tunes and older popular songs with a Western influence.

After the performance, many people from the audience patted our shoulders or pounded our backs, giving all six of us greater encouragement and making us feel very special. Later that night, after we had returned home, Tato continued to sing in his bed until he could stay awake no longer; his voice grew softer and softer until it finally faded, and he drifted off to sleep.

In my hometown, the day of a boy's circumcision was one of great significance, as important as one's birthday or wedding day, the anniversary of a person's death or even a public holiday. Although my mother had sent out no formal invitations, news of the ceremony had spread far and wide, and she received contributions to the event from all parts of town.

As was usually the case with major life rituals, we woke up extra-early on the day of our circumcisions, even though we had stayed up late the night before; by four-thirty in the morning, the house was already very busy. The candidates for circumcision bathed, and were then dressed in their new *kains*, adding a prayer-cap or headcloth. My sisters wore new clothes, and my mother dressed in a new *kain* too; hers had a *parang rusak* motif. For a top, she wore a long blouse with embroidered lapels and edging, a gift from an aunt who taught at the girls' school in Rembang. A green rainbow-motif shoulder sash completed her outfit.

My father had on his school uniform: a wraparound *kain* with a broken-dagger motif that matched my mother's, and a long-sleeved, button-up jacket. As usual, he was barefoot. (My father never wore shoes; only at home might he sometimes wear wooden cloppers or sandals.)

As if infected by my family's state of readiness, our neighbours rose early, too. All dressed in new clothing as well, they gathered at our house to escort us about a half kilometre away to school, where the ceremony was to be held.

Inside the school, a small tent-like shelter with sides made of mosquito netting had been erected for the circumcision ceremony. The six of us who were to be circumcised occupied a row of chairs nearby. As the hour of the ceremony approached, the number of visitors around the shelter grew larger, and comprised both adults and children. The girls remained at a slight distance.

Finally, a circumcision specialist – the *calak* – arrived, and proceeded to unwrap three straight-edge blades from their handkerchief covers. As he was doing this, an older man approached to offer words of advice: "Don't be afraid. It won't hurt. It's a bit like being bitten by a red ant. I laughed when I was circumcised."

His was only one of many comforting voices; but no matter how reassuring the tone, we couldn't completely expunge our anxiety and fear.

Then the ceremony began. My father and mother, who were seated on a pair of large chairs amongst the crowd of visitors, rose and approached the netted shelter. Pride and elation showed on their faces.

The first boy to enter the hut was my parents' foster son, the sixteen-year old, because he was the oldest. The other foster son, the one who had refused to be circumcised, was nowhere to be seen in the crowd. The children who had come to witness the ceremony crowded so close to the shelter that the adults were forced to shoo them away.

I was incredibly scared. I wanted to be a good Muslim, but that wasn't enough to still my terror.

And when the *calak* suddenly began to bawl out an incomprehensible prayer, the pounding of my heart in my chest grew that much stronger. When my foster brother was led out of the hut, he could scarcely walk. His face was drained of blood, and his lips looked almost white. He had no strength. The ushers seated him in his chair and placed a large earthenware saucer between his legs. It was filled with fine ash from the kitchen hearth to sop up the blood that was dripping from his penis.

One by one, the older boys entered the shelter. As with my foster brother, when they re-emerged from the hut their faces were pale, and they walked with unsteady gaits. As I stood up to enter the tent, I felt several people take hold of my shoulders, as if they were afraid I would try to run away. I was then ushered inside the hut. The *calak* was waiting there impatiently, with a ferocious gleam in his eye – at least that's how he appeared to me.

I was placed in a chair and my head was pulled

backward, so that I was now facing up toward the roof of the tent. While one of the ushers, an older man, held my shoulders tightly to steady me, another pair of old hands attached themselves to my temples so that I could not look down. Below me, on the floor, was another earthenware bowl filled with ash. I felt a hand grope my penis, and then my foreskin being twisted tightly until it began to sting and feel very hot. Just at that moment, a razor severed that knot of my skin. It was over; I was circumcised. The old man who had been holding my temples back released his hands. I looked down to see blood dripping from the end of my penis.

"Don't move," one of the men said.

"You have to wait until the first flow of blood has stopped," another added.

I stared at the stream of blood – a blackened cord as it began to coagulate – and watched it as it slowly fell and disappeared into the fine ash in the bowl directly below.

CIRCUMCISION

Because Tato was the youngest, he was the last to be circumcised, and when his operation was over he, too, was led out from the shelter and put back on the seat beside me. Blood continued to drip into the earthenware dishes beneath our legs. All eyes were upon us. Mother came to me and kissed my cheeks; her display of affection caused tears to well in my eyes. She kissed Tato on the cheek, too. Then father came over to congratulate us: "Well done, well done."

The visitors began to take their leave: first the children, and then, after them, the adults, one by one. After that, the six of us who had just been circumcised made our way home on foot as well.

We were treated like kings that day. Our wishes were commands. The families of the two poor boys who had also been circumcised came to our home bearing gifts of chicken and rice.

"Now that you've been circumcised, do you feel that something's changed?" my mother asked me.

"I feel really happy," I told her.

"And do you feel like a true Muslim?" she enquired.

Her question gave me pause; the fact was, I didn't feel any different. "I feel like I did yesterday," I tried to explain, "and the day before. I still don't feel like a true Muslim."

"Could it be because you don't perform the daily prayers?" Mother then asked.

"No, I always do all five," I told her.

"Your grandfather's been to Makkah. Maybe if you made the pilgrimage, you'd feel the change, and know that you were a true Muslim."

"Would we go by ship?" Tato chirped.

"Yes, you'd sail to Arabia," Mother answered.

"Wouldn't we have to be really rich to do that?" I wondered.

"Yes, you would," Mother said.

And with that, all my hopes of becoming a true Muslim vanished. I knew that my parents weren't well off, and that we could never afford to make the pilgrimage.

"Why hasn't Father ever been to Makkah?" I asked.

"Because your father doesn't have the money."

Although I suddenly wanted to be wealthy, I also knew that this would never be the case. And after I had healed, the thought of becoming a true Muslim never again entered my mind.

Titles from Paper + Ink

Visit **www.paperand.ink** to subscribe and receive the other books
by post, as well as to keep up to date about new volumes in the series.